PowerKids Readers:

The Bilingual Library of the United States of America™

Bilingual Edition
English / Spanish
Edición bilingüe

TENNESSEE

VANESSA BROWN

TRADUCCIÓN AL ESPAÑOL: MARÍA CRISTINA BRUSCA

The Rosen Publishing Group's
PowerKids Press™ & **Editorial Buenas Letras**™
New York

Published in 2006 by The Rosen Publishing Group, Inc.
29 East 21st Street, New York, NY 10010

First Edition

Layout Design: Thomas Somers
Photo Credits: Cover, pp. 9, 31 (Mountain) © David Muench/Corbis; pp. 5, 26 © Ralf-Finn Hestoft/Corbis; p. 7 © 2002 Geoatlas; p. 11, 31 (Village) © Lindsay Hebberd/Corbis; pp. 13, 31 (Rudolph) © Bettmann/Corbis; p 15 © Archivo Iconografico, S.A./Corbis; pp. 17, 31 (Crockett) © Burstein Collection/Corbis; p.19 © Tami Chappell/Reuters/Corbis; p. 21 © William Manning/Corbis; p.23 © www.freshairphoto.com; pp. 25, 30 (Capital) © Raymond Gehman/Corbis; p. 30 (Iris) © Josh Westrich/zefa/Corbis; p. 30 (Mockingbird) © D. Robert & Lorri Franz/Corbis; p.30 (Tulip poplar) © Lee Snider/Photo Images/Corbis; p. 31 (Smith) © Underwood & Underwood/Corbis; p.31(Haley) © Alex Gotfryd/Corbis; p. 31 (Gore) © Reuters/Corbis; p. 31 (Hiking) © Patrik Giardino/Corbis; p. 31 (Summit) © Patrick Murphy-Racey/NBAE via Getty Images

Brown, Vanessa, 1963–
    Tennessee / Vanessa Brown ; traducción al español, María Cristina Brusca.— 1st ed.
        p. cm. — (The bilingual library of the United States of America)
    Includes bibliographical references and index.
    ISBN 1-4042-3108-0 (library binding)
    1. Tennessee—Juvenile literature. I. Title. II. Series.
    F436.3.B76 2006
    976.8-dc22
                                                        2005026288

Manufactured in the United States of America

Due to the changing nature of Internet links, Editorial Buenas Letras has developed an online list of Web sites related to the subject of this book. This site is updated regularly. Please use this link to access the list:

http://www.buenasletraslinks.com/ls/tennessee

Contents

Contenido

Welcome to Tennessee

These are the flag and seal of the state of Tennessee. Captain LeRoy Reeves designed the flag. Reeves was a member of the Tennessee army.

Bienvenidos a Tennessee

Estos son la bandera y el escudo de Tennessee. LeRoy Reeves, capitán del ejército de Tennessee, fue el creador de la bandera.

Tennessee Flag and State Seal
_____
Bandera y escudo de Tennessee

Tennessee Geography

Tennessee is in the southeastern United States. Tennessee borders the states of Alabama, Mississippi, Arkansas, Missouri, Kentucky, Virginia, Georgia, and North Carolina.

Geografía de Tennessee

Tennessee está en el sureste de los Estados Unidos. Tennessee linda con los estados de Alabama, Misisipi, Arkansas, Misuri, Kentucky, Virginia, Georgia y Carolina del Norte.

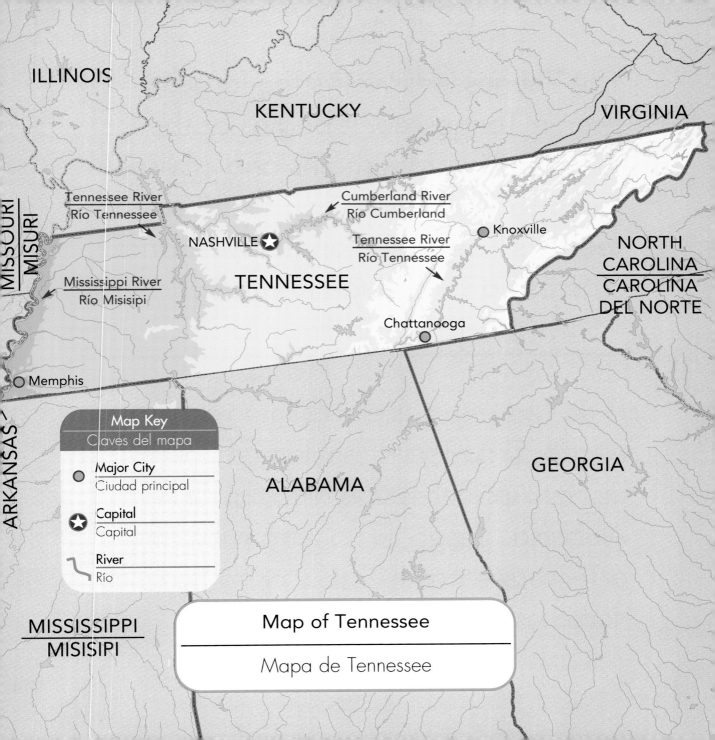

ILLINOIS

KENTUCKY

VIRGINIA

MISSOURI
MISURI

Tennessee River
Río Tennessee

Cumberland River
Río Cumberland

○ Knoxville

NASHVILLE ★

Tennessee River
Río Tennessee

NORTH
CAROLINA
CAROLINA
DEL NORTE

Mississippi River
Río Misisipi

TENNESSEE

Chattanooga
○

ARKANSAS

○ Memphis

Map Key
Claves del mapa

○ Major City
Ciudad principal

★ Capital
Capital

River
Río

GEORGIA

ALABAMA

MISSISSIPPI
MISISIPI

Map of Tennessee

Mapa de Tennessee

The Tennessee River is the largest river in Tennessee. It begins at the Appalachian Mountains and crosses south to Alabama. Then the river reenters Tennessee on the west and crosses north through Kentucky!

El río Tennessee es el más largo del estado. El río Tennessee nace en los montes Apalaches y se dirige al sur hasta Alabama. ¡Luego, el río entra nuevamente a Tennessee por el oeste y cruza hacia el norte hasta llegar a Kentucky!

The Tennessee River

Río Tennessee

Tennessee History

Three groups of Native Americans lived in Tennessee in the 1500s. These are the Creek, the Chickasaw, and the Cherokee. The state is named after Tenasie, a Cherokee village.

Historia de Tennessee

Tres grupos de nativos americanos vivían en Tennessee en los años 1500, los Creek, los Chickasaw y los Cheroquí. El nombre del estado viene del nombre de la aldea cheroquí Tenasie.

Native American Village Houses

Chozas en una aldea nativoamericana

Tennessee is known as the Volunteer State. This is because many Tennesseeans offered to fight against the British in the War of 1812. To volunteer means to offer help or to do a job.

Tennessee se conoce como el Estado de los Voluntarios. Este mote se debe a que muchos tennesianos se ofrecieron a luchar como voluntarios en contra de los británicos, en la Guerra de 1812. Ser un voluntario quiere decir ofrecerse para ayudar o para hacer un trabajo.

A Painting of the War of 1812

Una escena de la Guerra de 1812

Andrew Jackson was born in 1767. He became Tennessee's congressman and senator. Jackson was the seventh president of the United States, serving from 1829 to 1837.

Andrew Jackson nació en 1767. Representó a su estado como diputado y senador. Jackson llegó a ser el séptimo presidente de los Estados Unidos, sirviendo desde 1829 hasta 1837.

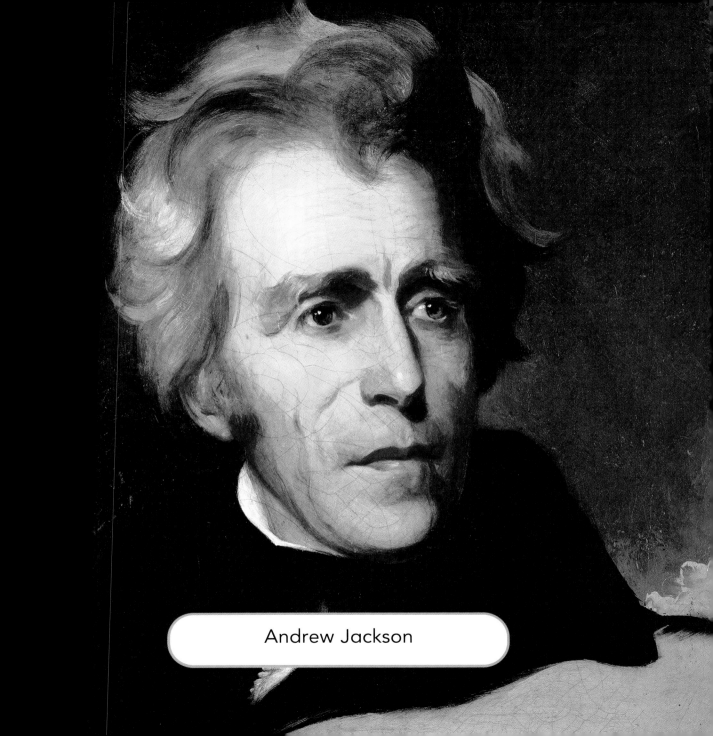

Andrew Jackson

Sequoyah was born in 1760 in the Tennessee mountains. Sequoyah wanted to find a way to write the Cherokee language. Back then the Cherokee language was only spoken. He created the Cherokee alphabet.

Sequoyah nació en 1760, en las montañas de Tennessee. En ese entonces, el idioma cheroquí era solamente hablado. Sequoyah buscó una manera de escribirlo y creó el alfabeto cheroquí.

Sequoyah Showing the Cherokee Alphabet

Sequoyah muestra el alfabeto cheroquí.

Living in Tennessee

Music is important in Tennessee. Many types of music, such as country music, rock and roll, and blues started in Tennessee. The capital of the state, Nashville, is known as Music City, USA.

La vida en Tennessee

La música es muy importante en Tennessee. Muchos tipos de música, como el *rock and roll*, la música *country* y los *blues*, comenzaron en Tennessee. La capital del estado, Nashville, es conocida como *Music City, USA.*

Concert at the Grand Ole Opry, in Tennessee

Concierto en el Grand Ole Opry, en Tennessee

Great Smoky National Park is the most-visited national park in the United States. About half of the park is in Tennessee. The other half is in North Carolina. People enjoy camping and hiking in the park.

El Parque Nacional Great Smoky es el más visitado de los Estados Unidos. La mitad de este parque está en Tennessee y la otra mitad en Carolina del Norte. Los visitantes disfrutan de acampar y dar caminatas por el parque.

Great Smoky Mountains National Park

Parque Nacional Great Smoky

Every year storytellers from all over the world come to Jonesborough, Tennessee, to tell their stories. Jonesborough has been the home of the Storytelling Festival for more than 30 years.

Cada año, narradores de cuentos de todo el mundo llegan a Jonesborough, Tennessee, para contar sus historias. Jonesborough ha sido el hogar del Festival de Narradores por más de treinta años.

Storytelling Festival in Jonesborough

Festival de narradores en Jonesborough

Memphis, Nashville, Knoxville, and Chattanooga are important cities in Tennessee. Nashville is the capital of the state.

Memphis, Nashville, Knoxville y Chattanooga son ciudades importantes de Tennessee. Nashville es la capital del estado.

Tennessee State Capitol Building

Capitolio del estado de Tennessee

Activity:
Let's Draw Tennessee's Flag

Actividad:
Dibujemos la bandera de Tennessee

1

Draw a rectangle.

Dibuja un rectángulo.

2

Draw two lines on the right side of the rectangle.

Traza dos líneas en el costado derecho del rectángulo.

26

3

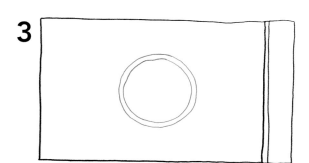

Draw two circles in the center of the rectangle.

Dibuja dos círculos en el centro del rectángulo.

4

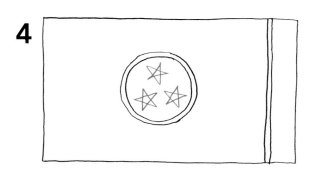

Add three stars inside the circles.

Agrega tres estrellas adentro de los círculos.

5

Erase extra lines and color in your flag.

Borra las líneas que no hagan falta y colorea tu bandera.

Timeline		Cronología
Hernando de Soto searches for gold around Tennessee.	**1540**	Hernando de Soto busca oro en la región de Tennessee.
Tennessee becomes the 16th state in the United States.	**1796**	Tennessee se convierte en el estado dieciseis de los Estados Unidos.
The United States forces the Cherokee out of their land.	**1836**	Los Estados Unidos arrojan a los cheroquíes de sus tierras.
A scientist in Tennessee begins work on the atomic bomb.	**1942**	Un científico, en Tennessee, comienza a trabajar en una bomba atómica.
Martin Luther King Jr. is killed in Memphis.	**1968**	Martin Luther King Jr. es asesinado, en Memphis.
The World's Fair takes place in Knoxville.	**1982**	La Exposición Mundial tiene lugar en Knoxville.
Al Gore Jr. runs for president of the United States.	**2000**	Al Gore Jr. es candidato a la presidencia de los Estados Unidos.

Tennessee Events

January
Elvis Presley Birthday Celebration,
in Memphis

April
Dogwood Arts Festival, in Knoxville

May
Rhythm in the Hills, in Sevierville

July
Fourth of July Midnight Parade,
in Gatlinburg

August-September
Tennessee Walking Horse National
Celebration, in Shelbyville

September
Farm Arts Festival, in Greeneville
Tennessee Fall Crafts Fair, in Nashville

October
Bluegrass Fan Fest, in Nashville

November
Tellabration—A Celebration of
Storytelling, in Greeneville
Trail of Tears Memorial Ride,
in Pulaski

Eventos en Tennessee

Enero
Celebración del cumpleaños de Elvis
Presley, en Memphis

Abril
Festival Dogwood de las artes, en Knoxville

Mayo
Ritmo en las colinas, en Sevierville

Julio
Desfile de medianoche del 4 de julio, en
Gatlinburg

Agosto-septiembre
Celebración nacional equina
en Shelbyville

Septiembre
Festival de las artes agrícolas, en Greenville
Feria de otoño de las artes, en Nashville

Octubre
Festival de aficionados al bluegrass,
en Nashville

Noviembre
Tellabration—Celebración de la narración
de cuentos, en Greenville
Cabalgata conmemorativa del Sendero
de las lágrimas, en Pulaski

Tennessee Facts/Datos sobre Tennessee

Population
5.6 million

Población
5.6 millones

Capital
Nashville

Capital
Nashville

State Motto
Agriculture and Commerce

Lema del estado
Agricultura y comercio

State Flower
Iris

Flor del estado
Lirio

State Bird
Mockingbird

Ave del estado
Sinsonte

State Nickname
Volunteer State

Mote del estado
Estado de los
Voluntarios

State Tree
Tulip poplar

Árbol del estado
Tulipero

State Song
"My Homeland Tennessee"

Canción del estado
"Mi hogar está en
Tennessee"

Famous Tennesseeans/Tennesianos famosos

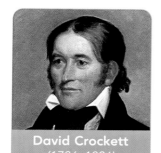

David Crockett
(1786–1836)

Frontiersman

Pionero

Bessie Smith
(1894–1937)

Blues singer

Cantante de *blues*

Alex Haley
(1921–1992)

Writer

Escritor

Wilma Rudolph
(1940–1994)

Olympic runner

Corredora olímpica

Al Gore Jr.
(1948–   )

U.S. vice president

Vicepresidente de los E.U.A

Pat Head Summit
(1952–   )

Basketball coach

Entrenadora de baloncesto

Words to Know/Palabras que debes saber

border
frontera

hiking
caminatas

mountain
montaña

village
aldea

Here are more books to read about Tennessee:
Otros libros que puedes leer sobre **Tennessee**:

In English/En inglés:

Tennessee
America the Beautiful Second Series
by Kent, Deborah
Children's Press, 2001

Tennessee
This Land Is Your Land
by Heinrichs, Ann
Compass Point Books, 2003

Words in English: 320

Palabras en español: 352

Index

Índice